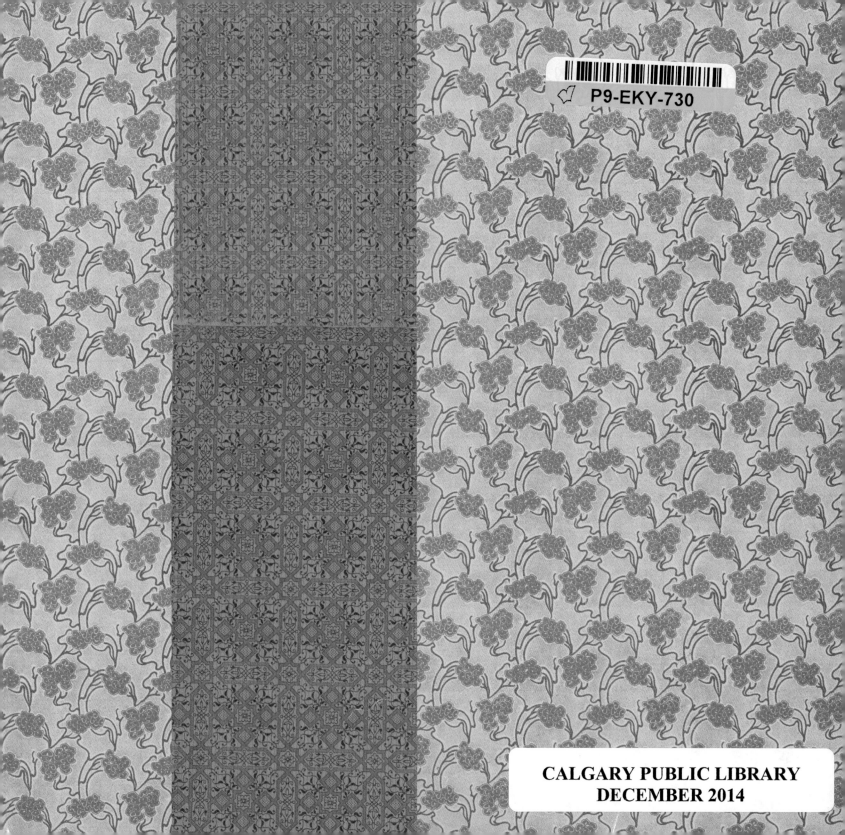

Mia's Thumb

LJUBA STILLE

Holiday House / New York

Mia sucked her thumb.
It comforted her when
she was sad.

It calmed her when she was excited about presents on the other side of the door.

It rescued her when Mrs. Smith said, "He just wants to play!"

And it encouraged her when
she needed to be brave.

Mia needed her
thumb when a
movie was too
exciting . . .

or too boring. In short, Mia loved her thumb!

"Stop it!" Mommy said.
"You are too big for that!"

At times like that, Mia
still wanted to be small,
and she continued to
suck her thumb.

"Stop it!" Daddy said.
"Your teeth will get
crooked!"

But Mia didn't think that
crooked teeth were quite
so bad, and she continued
to suck her thumb.

"Stop it!" said her brother, Paul.
"It's really embarrassing!"

But Mia was too young to be embarrassed, so she continued to suck her thumb.

"Talk doesn't work," said Grandpa. "Only bribery works. I will give you a lot of money if you stop."

But Mia didn't know what to do with a lot of money.

Daddy had an idea. He drew a little king on Mia's finger. Daddy thought that Mia wouldn't want to put a little king in her mouth.

"The little king tastes nice," Mia said, and he soon disappeared.

Grandma had been watching,
but she hadn't said
anything until now.
"If you stop sucking
your thumb for half
an hour, I'll buy you
an ice cream cone." It worked.

But it stopped working
after the seventh cone.

"There must be
something very special
about sucking one's
thumb," Grandma said.
"I'll try it!"

So Grandma sucked her thumb.
"Stop it!" Daddy said. "Your teeth will get crooked!"

"Then I'll take my teeth out!" Grandma said, and she continued to suck her thumb.

"Stop it!" said Grandpa. "Or I'll run away from home!"

"Go ahead," said Grandma, who knew full well that Grandpa would never do such a thing. She continued to suck her thumb.

"Stop it!" Mia said. "It's really embarrassing!" But Grandma was too old to be embarrassed, so she continued to suck her thumb.

Text and illustrations by Ljuba Stille
Copyright © 2013 by Kinderbuchverlag Wolff GmbH
First published in Germany in 2013 as LIESE LUTSCHT
by Kinderbuchverlag Wolff GmbH, Frankfurt am Main
First published in the United States in 2014 by Holiday House, New York
English translation copyright © 2014 by Anja Mundt
This edition is published by arrangement with mundt agency, Germany

Library of Congress Cataloging-in-Publication Data
Stille, Ljuba, author, illustrator.
Mia's thumb / Ljuba Stille ; English translation by Anja Mundt. — First edition.
pages cm
"First published in Germany in 2013 as LIESE LUTSCHT by Kinderbuchverlag Wolff GmbH, Frankfurt am Main."
Summary: Mia's family members, from her brother to her grandparents,
try all they can think of to get her to stop sucking her thumb.
ISBN 978-0-8234-3067-3 (hardcover)
[1. Thumb sucking—Fiction. 2. Family life—Fiction.] I. Mundt, Anja, translator. II. Title.
PZ7.S8566Mi 2014
[E]—dc23
2013037255

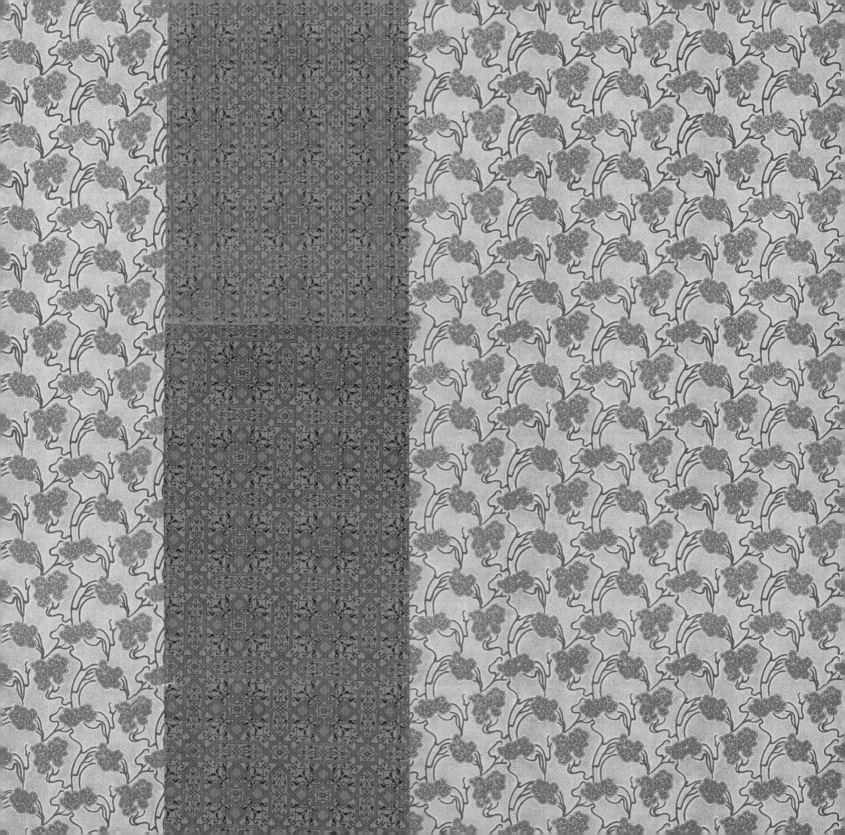

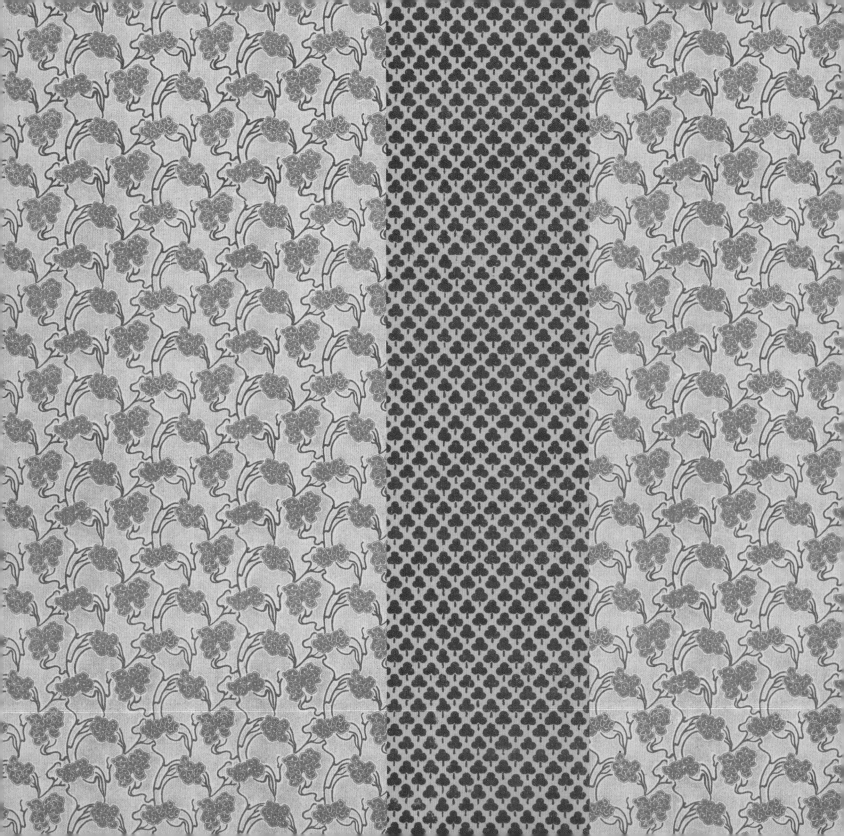